This book belongs to:

You're Too

For Sadie Littlejohn – Gordon, Kevin and Robert's SuperMum S.P.

YOU'RE TOO BIG! A PICTURE CORGI BOOK 0 552 54828 6
First published in Great Britain by Doubleday, an imprint of Random House Children's Books Doubleday edition published 2003. Picture Corgi edition published 2004.
1 3 5 7 9 10 8 6 4 2

RANDOM HOUSE CHILDREN'S BOOKS 61–63 Uxbridge Rd, London W5 5SA. A division of The Random House Group Ltd. RANDOM HOUSE AUSTRALIA (PTY) LTD 20 Alfred Street, Milsons Point, Sydney, New South Wales 2061, Australia RANDOM HOUSE NEW ZEALAND LTD 18 Poland Road, Glenfield, Auckland 10, New Zealand RANDOM HOUSE (PTY) LTD Endulini, 5A Jubilee Road, Parktown 2193, South Africa THE RANDOM HOUSE GROUP Limited Reg. No. 954009 www.kidsatrandomhouse.co.uk A CIP catalogue record for this book is available from the British Library.
Printed in Singapore.

BIG!

Simon Puttock

Illustrated by

Emily Bolam

PICTURE CORGI

It was Elephant's first day at Playschool,
and he was feeling very new.
"What would you like to do?" asked Mrs Gnu.
"Blocks!" said Elephant, ambling over to Lion,
but CRASH! Lion's blocks went flying.

"How about a nice quiet book?" suggested Mrs Gnu.

Elephant sat next to Hyena. But SQUASH! he sat on Hyena's best book and bent it right in two.

squash!

Mouse was doing brilliant pawprints.
"Pictures are a good staying-still sort of thing,"
said Mrs Gnu kindly.
"I can paint with my trunk," said Elephant,
but SPLODGE! he made a great big mark
on Mouse's painting.

splodge!

"GO AWAY, ELEPHANT!" she squeaked.
"You're too big and clumsy!"
Poor Elephant. He hadn't meant to do it.
"I think," said Mrs Gnu, "it's playtime now."

Elephant sat on the seesaw. "Who wants to go up and down?" he asked.
"Me first," said Mouse, and she climbed onto the other end.

Elephant waited. Mouse waited.
But nobody went up and down.
Lion climbed up next to Mouse.
And nobody went up and down.

Hyena climbed up next to Mouse and Lion.
Still nobody went up and down.
"You're TOO BIG, Elephant," said Mouse.
Poor Elephant felt quite small inside.

"Let's play on the swings," said Lion.
Everyone swung to and fro.
Everyone except Elephant.
"I think I need a push, please," he said.

Hyena pushed, but Elephant did not swing
to and fro.
Lion pushed Hyena pushing Elephant. But still
he did not swing to and fro.

Mouse pushed Lion pushing Hyena pushing
Elephant, but *still* he did not swing to and fro.
Suddenly CRACK! the swing broke, and Elephant
sat down BUMP!
"You're TOO BIG, Elephant," said Mouse.
Poor Elephant felt very small and sad inside.

"Let's play on the slide," said Hyena.
"I think Elephant had better go LAST," said Mouse.
So Elephant went last.
Elephant closed his eyes and started to slide.

He slid a VERY LITTLE WAY. Then he stuck. He couldn't go down and he couldn't go up. "Just as I expected," sighed Mouse. "Elephant, you're just TOO BIG."

Poor Elephant. "I'm not too big," he whispered. "I'm small." And a tear trickled down his trunk. "Small?" cried Mouse. "Elephant, you're TOO BIG and ENORMOUS!"

Elephant felt small and
sad and FED UP inside.

"I'm NOT, NOT, NOT!" he shouted. "You're too
LITTLE! I am just the right size, I know because
my mummy told me so!"

"I think," said Mrs Gnu, unsticking Elephant,
"that it's time for a song."
Elephant knew all the words,
and he sang them
beautifully loudly.

Everyone else stopped singing to listen.
"Oh dear," thought Elephant. "They're cross again."

But no-one was cross. Everyone was smiling.
"Oh, Elephant," said Mrs Gnu, "you have a
BEAUTIFUL singing voice."
"Do I?" asked Elephant, surprised.
"Yes," said Lion.
"Yes," said Hyena.

"Yes, you do," said Mouse. "It is a BIG voice, but it is beautiful too."

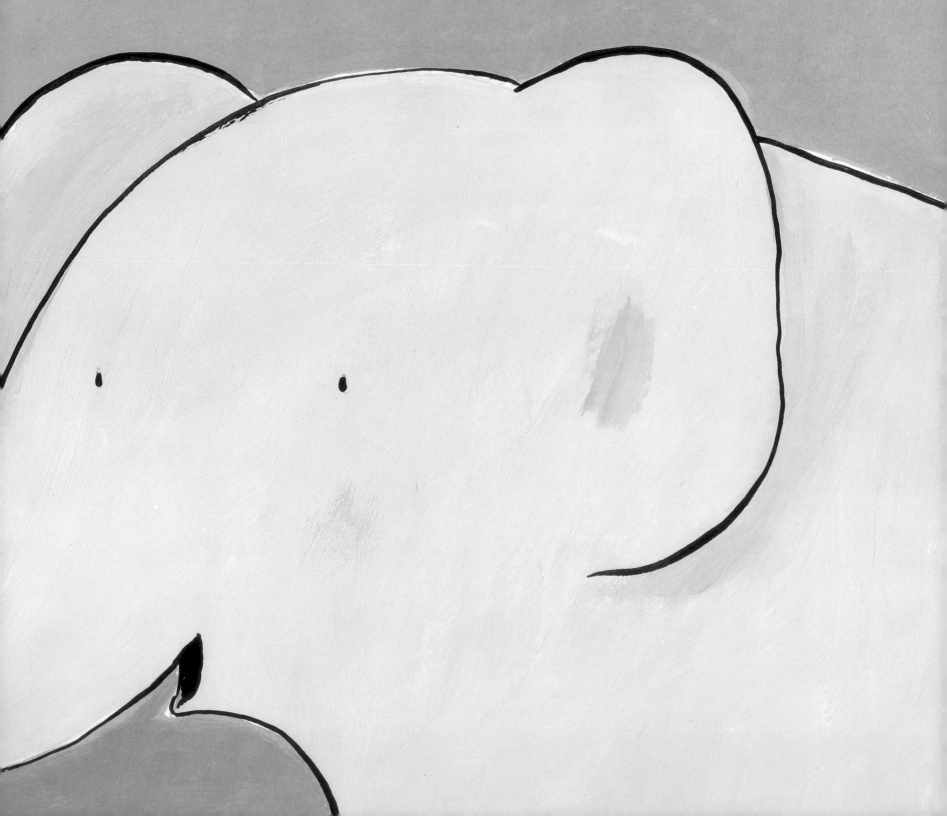

It was going home time. All the Mummies and Daddies were waiting for a cuddle.

Hyena got a wriggly, giggly cuddle.

Lion got a furry,
purry cuddle.

Mouse got a sniffy,
squeaky cuddle.

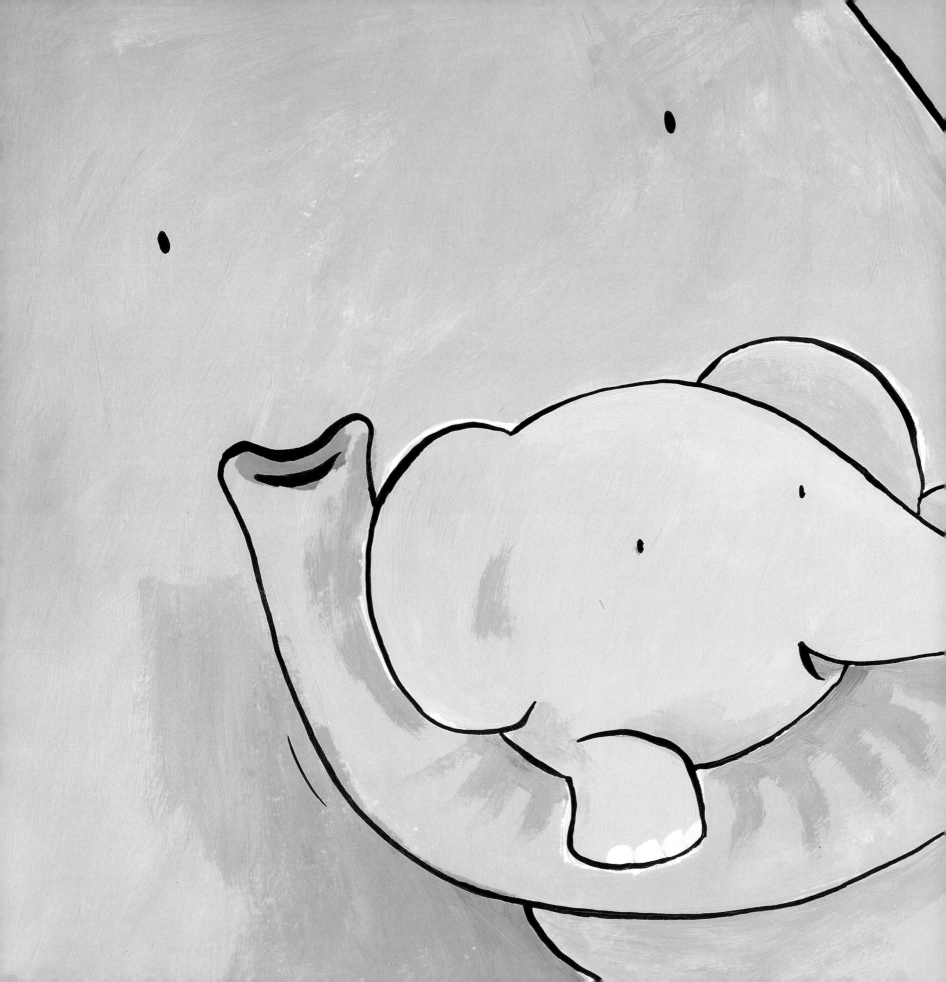

And Elephant's Mummy curled Elephant up in her long, loving trunk and gave him a big, ENORMOUS cuddle.
And everyone could see that Elephant really *was* just the right size after all.

Even Mouse.

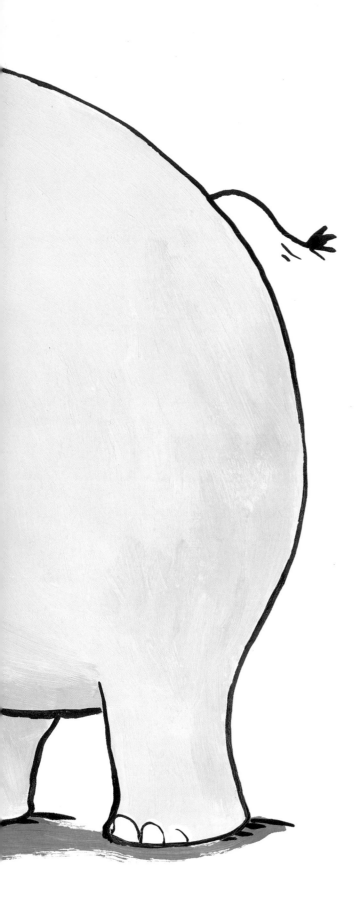

You're never too BIG for books!

Here are some books to share
with your friends:

Our Twitchy
by Kes Gray and Mary McQuillan

Squeaky Clean
by Simon Puttock and Mary McQuillan

Ahoyty-Toyty
by Helen Stephens

Who Will Sing My Puff-a-Bye?
by Charlotte Hudson and
Mary McQuillan